The Animated Menorah
CHANUKAH
Activity Book

Design and Graphics by **Janet Zwebner**

Based on the **Animated Menorah** book

Clay figures by **Rony Oren**

The Animated Menorah
CHANUKAH ACTIVITY BOOK

Published by **Scopus Films (London) Ltd.**
30 Cliff Road, London NW1 9AG
15 Efratah St., Jerusalem 93384

Distributed by

Shapolsky Publishers, Inc.,
136 W. 22nd St., New York, NY 10011

Printed and bound by **Keterpress Enterprises**
in Jerusalem, Israel.

10 9 8 7 6 5 4 3 2 1

ISBN 0-944007-61-9

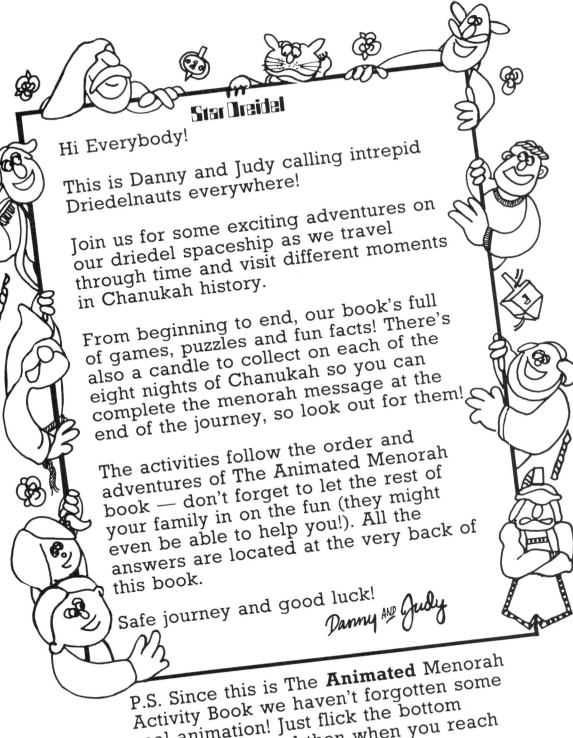

Star Dreidel

Hi Everybody!

This is Danny and Judy calling intrepid Driedelnauts everywhere!

Join us for some exciting adventures on our driedel spaceship as we travel through time and visit different moments in Chanukah history.

From beginning to end, our book's full of games, puzzles and fun facts! There's also a candle to collect on each of the eight nights of Chanukah so you can complete the menorah message at the end of the journey, so look out for them!

The activities follow the order and adventures of The Animated Menorah book — don't forget to let the rest of your family in on the fun (they might even be able to help you!). All the answers are located at the very back of this book.

Safe journey and good luck!

Danny AND Judy

P.S. Since this is The **Animated** Menorah Activity Book we haven't forgotten some real animation! Just flick the bottom page corners and then when you reach the end of the book, flick them backwards to see what happens to the Chanukah characters.

1

To activate the **Star Driedel** we have to find the secret password! Unscramble the words below and write them in the boxes. Then put each circled letter onto the keyboard above and unscramble once again to find the word you're looking for.

ONHAMER   GLIHT   TEGIH

KCUNHAAH   ERDLEID   AEBCMACE

ENALCD

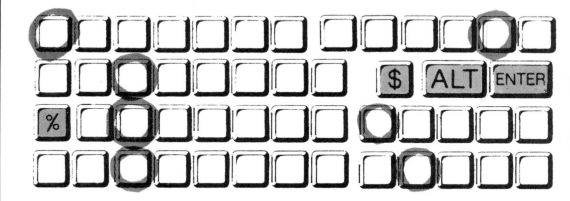

fun facts

Do you know what a **miracle** is? A miracle is something surprising and wonderful that happens — like when a little bit of oil lasted for eight whole days in the story of Chanukah. Can you think of another miracle?

2

Look for this man's name hidden in the picture.
Then draw him in and color the page.

Do you know
who this man is?

Candle 1

CLUE: His nickname is "The Madman".
He ordered idols put in the Temple and
sacrifices offered on the 25th
Kislev—exactly 3 years before the
Maccabee victory!

Using the color code on the opposite page,

fun facts

Mosaics are a very ancient form of art in which tiny bits of colored stone, tile or glass are stuck to a wall or floo in beautiful patterns very much like the ones you're working on in this book!

color in this original Temple mosaic.

RED YELLOW BLUE GREEN

YELLOW $\boxed{X}$ BLUE $\boxed{-}$ GREEN $\boxed{I}$

Complete this mosaic by tracing and coloring in each row of squares. Then carefully cut them out and stick them in the right places according to the color code you'll find here.

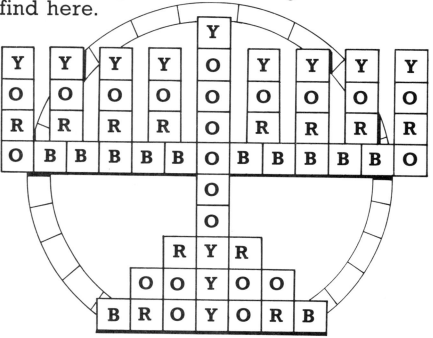

Y yellow   O orange   R red   B brown

Someone has been cutting up the photo album again! Look carefully to see what Chanukah objects are in each picture.

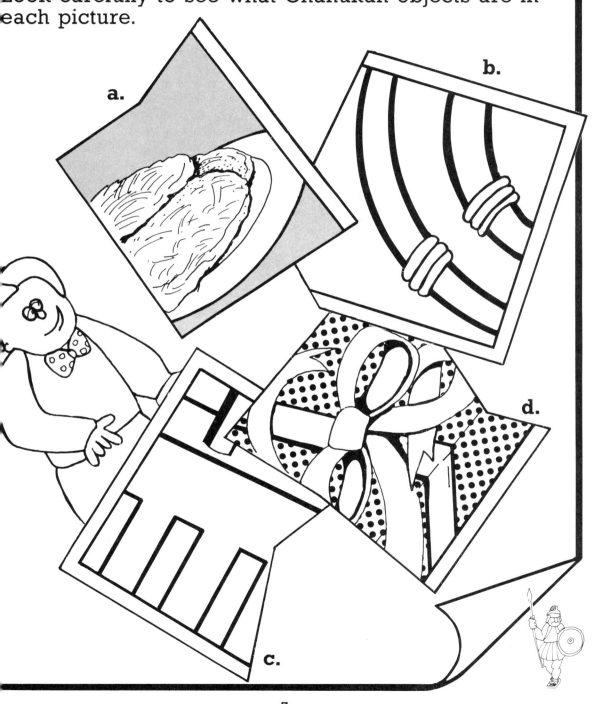

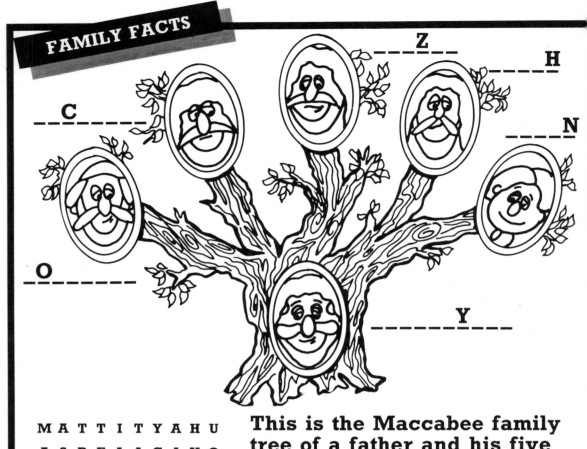

C _ _ _ _ _ _ _ _ _ _

Z _ _ _ _ _ _ _ _

H _ _ _ _ _

N _ _ _ _ _

O _ _ _ _ _ _ _ _

Y _ _ _ _ _ _ _

M A T T I T Y A H U
A S P E J J C I K Q
M I R D U W E B U Y
O M B O D Y L Y R E
Y O C H A N A N L V
Z N G X H F Z X W C
J O N A T H A N M V
O T U S A X R P D Z

This is the Maccabee family tree of a father and his five brave sons (their family name is Hasmonean). Find their names in this word puzzle and write them in the blanks on the tree. We've filled in a few letters to give you a head start.

NAME: _____

RANK: _____

NUMBER: _____

MISSION: _____

Photo

AS ONE OF THE MACCABEES YOU MUST CARRY AN IDENTITY CARD AT ALL TIMES!

Fill out the card and add a recent photo of yourself.

8

Make your own Maccabee battle plan to take Jerusalem! Use arrows to show which way you would send your army.

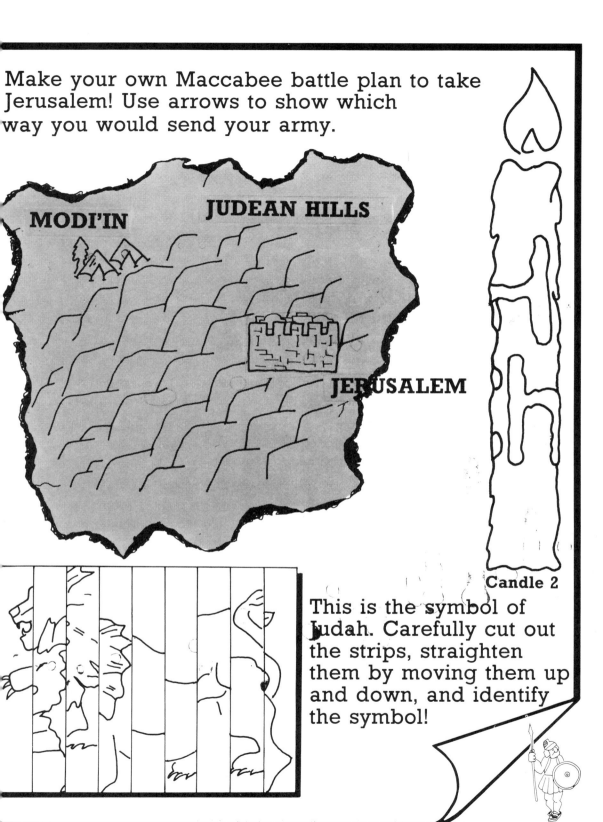

MODI'IN

JUDEAN HILLS

JERUSALEM

Candle 2

This is the symbol of Judah. Carefully cut out the strips, straighten them by moving them up and down, and identify the symbol!

9

Help Danny and Judy find their way out of the Maccabee hideout in the caves. Watch out! Don't get trapped by Greek soldiers, secret passages or dead-ends!

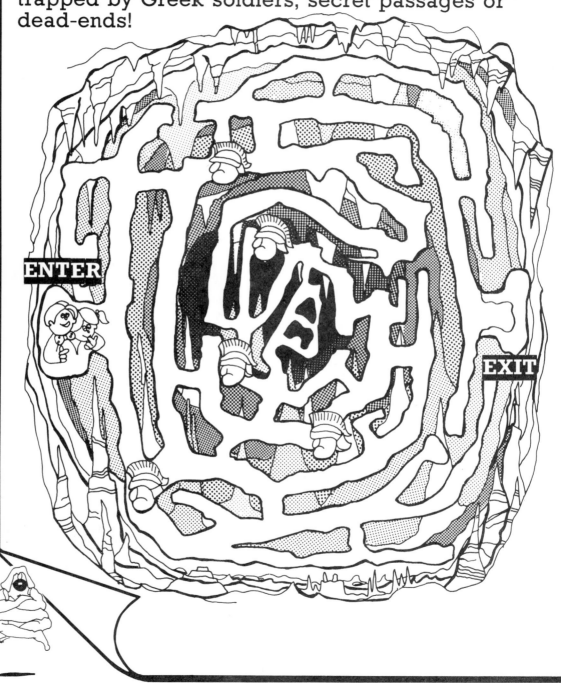

Color in this battle scene as the outnumbered Maccabees fight off the Greek soldiers.

un facts

Chanukah is our symbol of the miracle of victory. Throughout history there have many miracles in which the Jews have triumphed over terrible hardships. Can you think of some of these miracles?

11

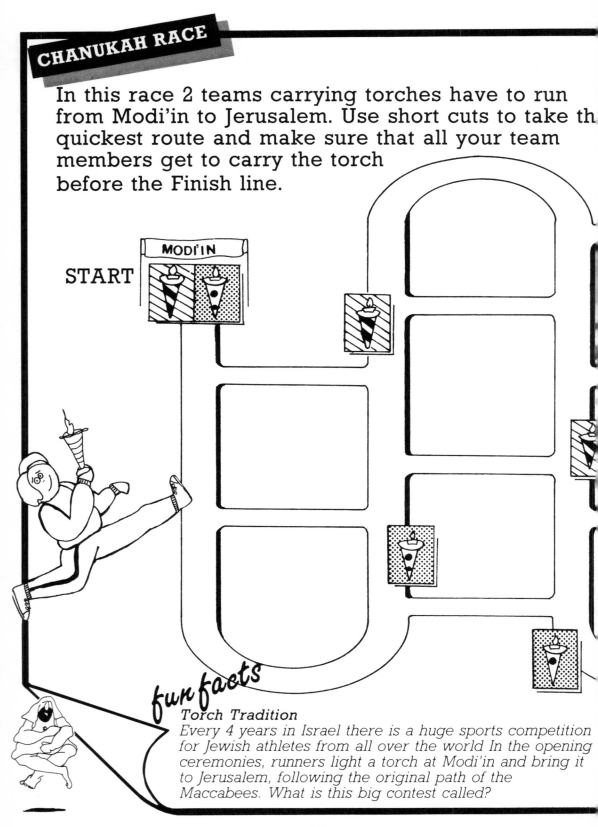

CHANUKAH RACE

In this race 2 teams carrying torches have to run from Modi'in to Jerusalem. Use short cuts to take the quickest route and make sure that all your team members get to carry the torch before the Finish line.

START MODI'IN

fun facts

Torch Tradition
Every 4 years in Israel there is a huge sports competition for Jewish athletes from all over the world In the opening ceremonies, runners light a torch at Modi'in and bring it to Jerusalem, following the original path of the Maccabees. What is this big contest called?

JERUSALEM FINISH

fun facts

Sneaky Greeks

The Greeks built a gym next to the Temple in Jerusalem, hoping to tempt the priests into playing games and sports instead of carrying out their religious duties.

What happened to Elazar Maccabee? Connect the dots and you'll find out!

fun facts

You might be wondering what happened to the other Maccabee brothers, Yochanan, Judah, Jonathan and Simon. Yochanan was killed by an Arabian tribe, Judah was killed in a battle against the Syrians and Jonathan was tricked and murdered by the Syrian general who pretended to be his friend. Simon, the only survivor, became a high priest. His sons carried on the Maccabee family fight.

The Maccabees need your help to find the last container of oil. Starting at one of the Temple gates you must also collect the eight Chanukah light holders on the way. Remember, you can only travel along the same route once!

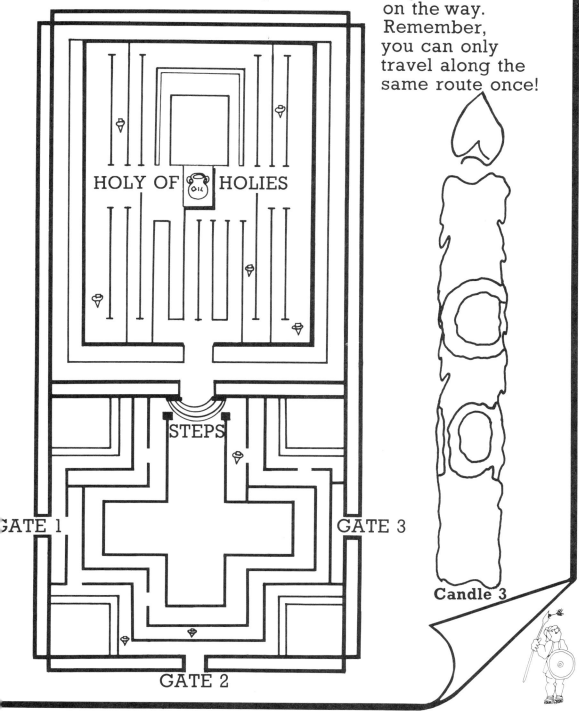

Candle 3

Imagine that there was once a newspaper in old Jerusalem called the **Judean Journal**. Write your news report of the Maccabee victory, and don't forget a headline and captions for the pictures!

Judean Journal
25th Kislev

_____

_____

BY _____

_____

_____

_____

_____

_____

_____

_____

_____

_____

_____

_____

_____

_____

_____

_____

_____

_____

fun facts

Chanukah means "to make holy or dedicate".
In Hebrew we write it like this: **חנוכה**
It can also be written **חנו·כ"ה**
meaning "they rested", which is exactly what the Maccabees did after their victory on the 25th.

ACROSS

1. The lion is the symbol of ----
2. Let's play ---- for Chanukah
3. Hebrew for driedel
4. The top of the candle
5. Home of the Marranos Jews
7. Kislev is the 3rd ---- in the Jewish calendar

8. The menorah should stand (close to) the window

DOWN

6. Another name for Maccabee
9. On the 1st night we light - candle
10. They used to --- oil in clay jars.

fun facts

The original Temple menorah had 7 branches, but because it was so holy we're not allowed to copy it. Instead we use menorahs with 5 or 6 branches, and 8 branches for Chanukah.

These evil Spanish inquisitors have go
strange things are happening. What's wro

fun facts

*Who were the Marranos? They were Jews living in Spa
over 400 years ago. The Marranos had to pretend to be
Christian in public, or they would have been captured
and killed by the soldiers of the Spanish Inquisition!*

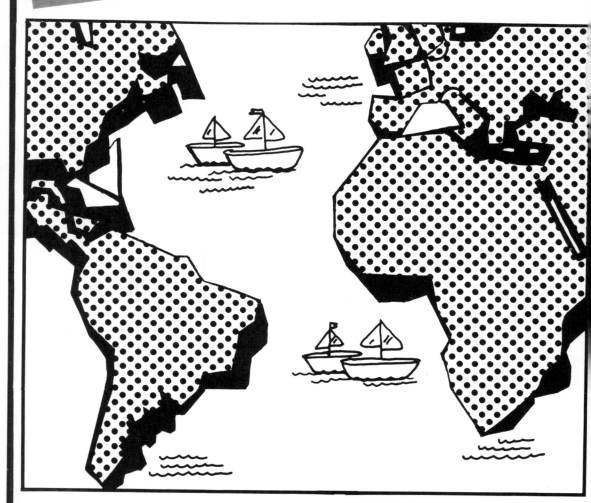

The Spanish Jews escaped from the Inquisition to find new homes in many different places. The map above shows where they went. Unscramble the names below and put them where they belong on the map.

PETYG   ALTIY   TSUOH   ERMCAAI

LNALHOD   RFCANE   OCROMCO

This portrait is of a very famous explorer who set sail for America the same day that the Spanish Inquisition started in 1492. The letters of his name are scattered around the picture. Gather them up and write his name in the plaque that you see below. Don't forget to color in his portrait!

Candle 4

fun facts

We know for sure that Christopher Columbus had many Jewish crew members on board his ships, but did you know that lots of people believe that Columbus himself was Jewish?

Pick out the odd dreidel from each row. Now, moving one word at a time, put the words of this famous saying in the right order.

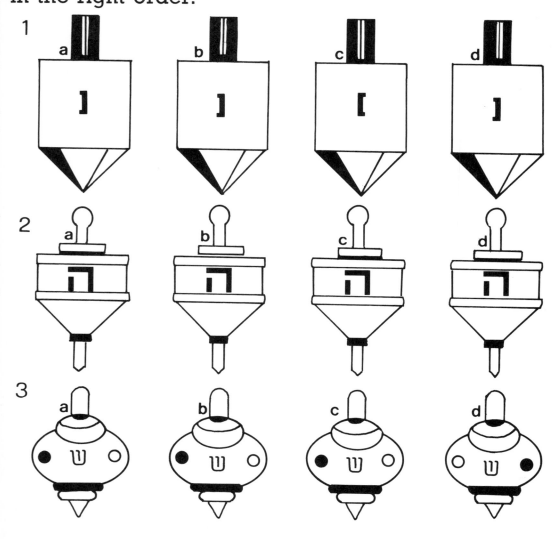

1 a b c d

2 a b c d

3 a b c d

fun facts

In Israel all the dreidels say "a great miracle happened **here**" (נס גדול היה פה) but in the rest of the world they say "a great miracle happened **there**" (נס גדול היה שם)!

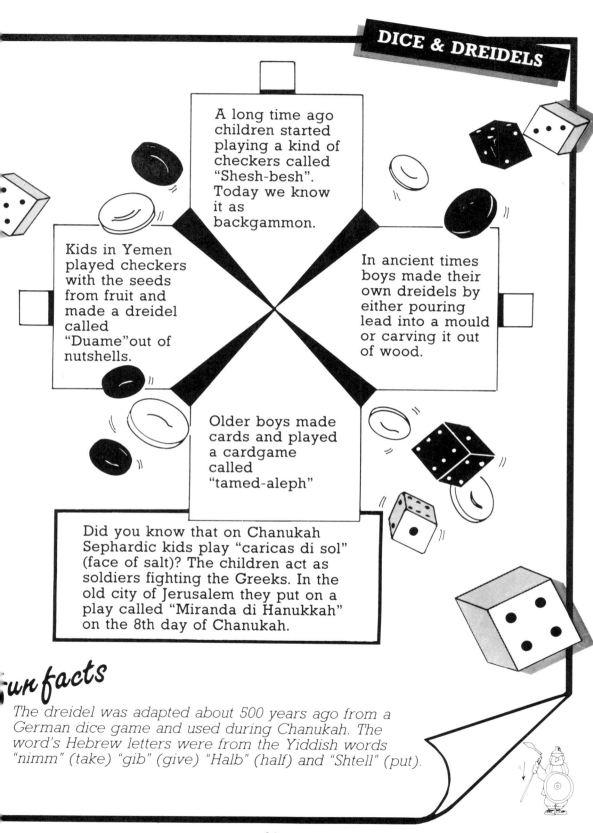

A long time ago children started playing a kind of checkers called "Shesh-besh". Today we know it as backgammon.

Kids in Yemen played checkers with the seeds from fruit and made a dreidel called "Duame" out of nutshells.

In ancient times boys made their own dreidels by either pouring lead into a mould or carving it out of wood.

Older boys made cards and played a cardgame called "tamed-aleph"

Did you know that on Chanukah Sephardic kids play "caricas di sol" (face of salt)? The children act as soldiers fighting the Greeks. In the old city of Jerusalem they put on a play called "Miranda di Hanukkah" on the 8th day of Chanukah.

Fun facts

The dreidel was adapted about 500 years ago from a German dice game and used during Chanukah. The word's Hebrew letters were from the Yiddish words "nimm" (take) "gib" (give) "Halb" (half) and "Shtell" (put).

JUDY'S JUGSAW

[TRACE] Color and cut out this jigsaw puzzle which shows Judy receiving her medal from George Washington.

24

Who is lighting the Chanukah candles here? Connect the dots and you'll find out!

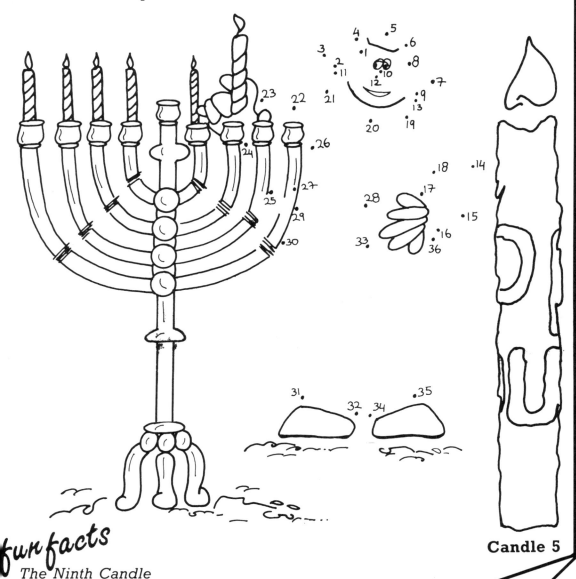

Candle 5

fun facts

The Ninth Candle
Chanukah candles are really just to look at and not to use, so we have another candle that we use both to light them and to give light. This ninth candle has a special name. Do you know what it is? (Answer below)

The Shammash

The song "Maoz Zur" was written about 600 years ago by a mysterious German poet. We only know his name because he spelled it out in the first letter of each verse. Find the 5 verses by straightening the candles into the correct order, then use the first letters to find his name. (Helpful hint: use a siddur to help you find the words to **"Maoz Zur"**)

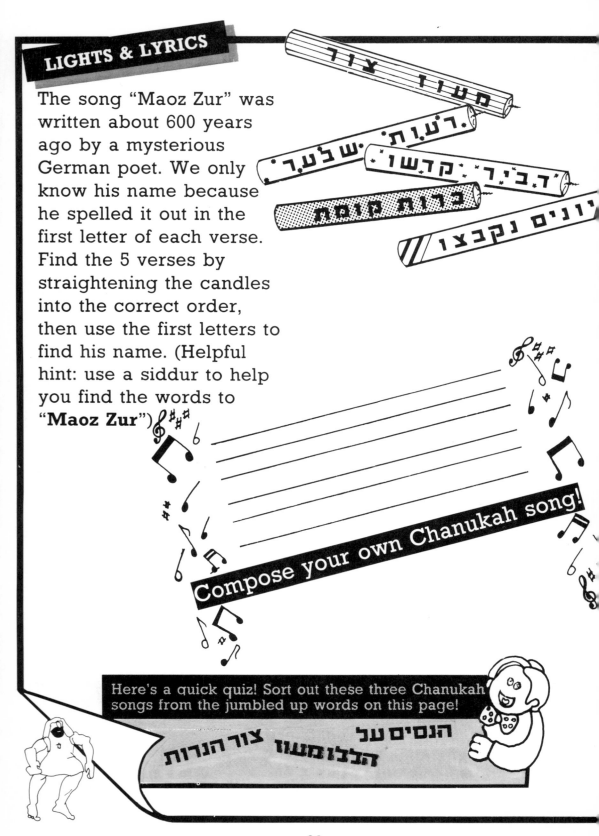

מעוז צור

רעות שלער

הביר קדשו

יונים נקבצו

Compose your own Chanukah song!

Here's a quick quiz! Sort out these three Chanukah songs from the jumbled up words on this page!

הנסים על הללו מעוז צור הנרות

Menorot come in all styles and materials
Guess what these menorot are made of!

UNSCRAMBLE THESE WORDS FOR CLUES

NEOTS   ADEL   SGLSA   SRBAS

OSTAPTO   RLSIVE   AYLC   ZRBOEN

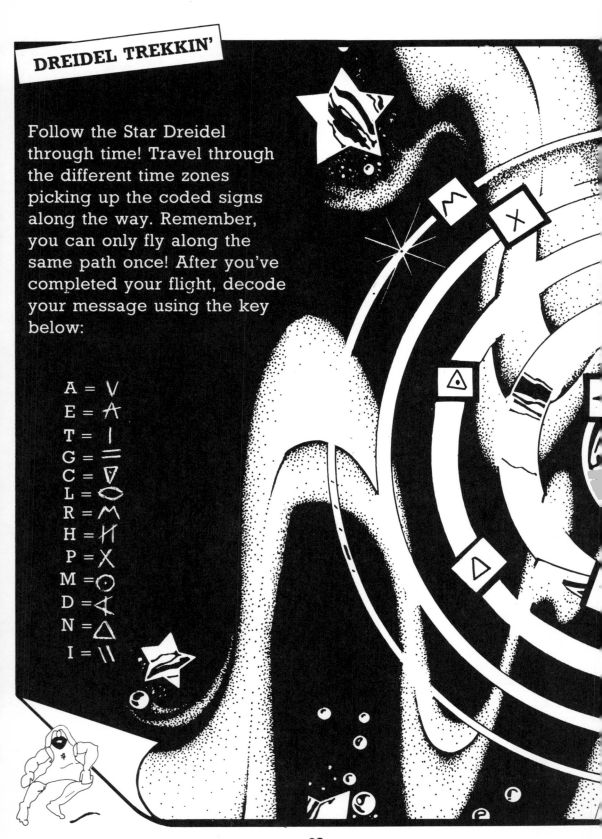

DREIDEL TREKKIN'

Follow the Star Dreidel through time! Travel through the different time zones picking up the coded signs along the way. Remember, you can only fly along the same path once! After you've completed your flight, decode your message using the key below:

A = V
E = A
T = |
G = =
C = V
L = O
R = M
H = H
P = X
M = ⊙
D = ◁
N = △
I = \\

Uncle Reuben is showing us some photos of hi
Moroccan rescue mission. Color in and caption
each picture.

Candle 6

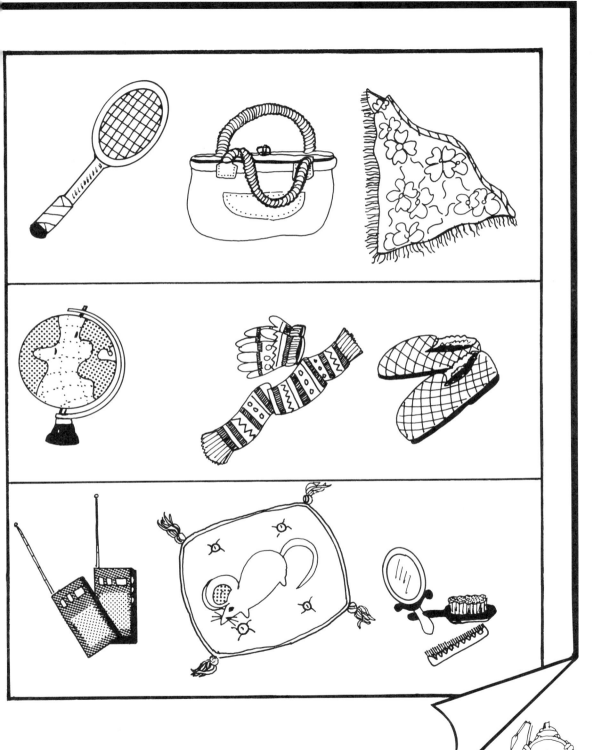

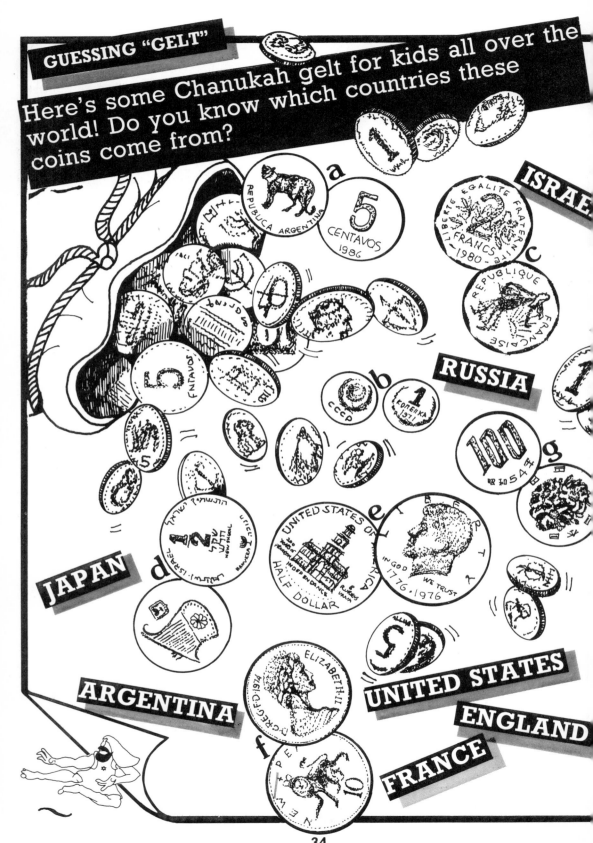

GUESSING "GELT"

Here's some Chanukah gelt for kids all over the world! Do you know which countries these coins come from?

ISRAEL

RUSSIA

JAPAN

ARGENTINA

UNITED STATES

FRANCE

ENGLAND

There are eight potatoes hidden in this picture. Find them so Larissa's father can make his menorah.

Candle 7

in facts

Do you know the name given to Russian Jews who are not allowed to leave Russia?

Answer: Refusenik

Write an original Chanukah adventure using the objects on this page. You can also use pictures and songs to illustrate your story.

CHANUKAH ADVENTURE!

By

_____

The end

1. **HISTORY** — What was Judah Maccabee's nickname?

2. **RELIGION** — In the Temple, on which side of the Ark did the Menorah stand?

3. **PEOPLE** — Which day of Chanukah is for women?

4. **CULTURE** — What type of civilization did the Greeks have?

5. **SPORTS** — What sports event is named after the competition started by the Greeks?

6. **SCIENCE** — What doesn't mix with water?

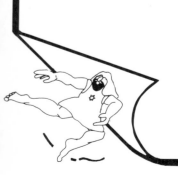

ANSWERS
1. "The Hammer" 2. The right side 3. The 7th 4. Hellenic 5. The Olympics 6. Oil

When you've collected the seven other candles put them together on this page and read the message!

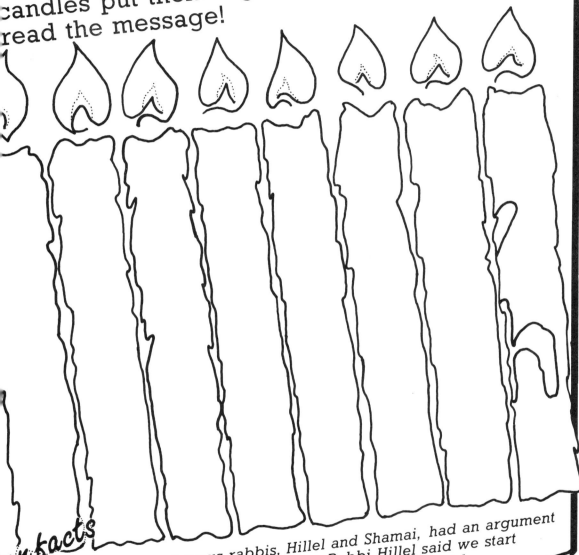

fun facts

Many years ago two famous rabbis, Hillel and Shamai, had an argument about how to light the Chanukah candles. Rabbi Hillel said we start with one candle and add to it each night. Rabbi Shamai said we should light eight candles first and then blow one out each night. In the end, we follow Rabbi Hillel, and light the candles one at a time as he suggested.

CHANUKAH CROSSWORD

ACROSS

2. What was the Temple menorah made of?
4. What lasted for eight days
6. A special nut for Chanukah
9. Chanukah begins ___ the 25th of Kislev
10. What God did on Chanukah
14. The part of the Temple
15. A potato pancake
16. "— Hanissim"
17. How do you say "shesh" in English?

DOWN

1. You always do it to birthday candles but never to Chanukah candles; _____ them out.
2. Chanukah money
3. _____ of Titus in Rome with a picture of a menorah on it
5. Antiochus put one in the temple
7. How many containers of oil did the Maccabees find in the Temple
8. "A (wonderful) miracle happened there"
10. A cast for a dreidel — also grows on cheese
11. Maccabee hillside hideouts
12. A wax stamp used to _____ a letter
13. Red earth; sometimes it was used to make menorot.
14. Candles are made of this

REMEMBER, GET HELP FROM AN ADULT BEFORE YOU START WORKING IN THE KITCHEN!

Star Driedel Potato Latkes

4 large potatoes
4 tbs self-rising flour
2 beaten eggs
1 tsp. salt
Pepper to taste
Oil for frying

1. Grate potatoes finely and sieve
2. Mix remaining ingredients and add to the potatoes
3. Carefully heat oil in pan
4. Put spoonfuls of the mixture in the oil
5. Fry for 5 minutes on each side and then drain on a paper towel

CHEF'S TIP

It might seem pretty impossible to get jelly on the inside of a doughnut, but it's not! Here are 3 different ways you can try:

1. While the doughnuts are still warm, make a little hole with a spoon and poke the jelly in. (Kinda messy, but remember, you can eat your mistakes!)
2. Squirt the jelly in with a pastry syringe or cake icing tube — this way's usually the easiest. If you don't have a cake icing tube you can make one by rolling a paper cone and squeezing the jelly out of the little end.

Chanukah Doughnuts

1 oz. dry yeast
1 tsp. sugar
1/4 cup warm water

2 cups flour
2 eggs
2 tbs sugar
1 cup warm water
Pinch of salt
1/2 tsp vanilla
Jelly
Oil for frying

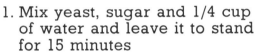

1. Mix yeast, sugar and 1/4 cup of water and leave it to stand for 15 minutes
2. Add all the other ingredients
3. Let the dough rise until it doubles in size
4. Shape it into balls
5. Fry them in oil until golden brown
6. Drain them on a paper towel
7. Fill each doughnut with jelly (see **Chef's Tip**)

3. Before you fry the dough put some jelly into each doughnut and roll the dough over it. Then let it rise again and fry it.

Israeli Chanukah "Sufganiyot"

2 cups self-rising flour
2 eggs
2 tbs. sugar
2 cups plain yogurt
1 pkg. vanilla sugar
A pinch of salt
Jelly
Powdered sugar
Oil for frying

1. Mix flour with eggs, yogurt, vanilla sugar and salt
2. Heat the oil in a deep pan
3. Carefully drop spoonfuls of the mixture into the oil
4. Cook until brown; drain on paper towels
5. Put jelly inside and roll the dougnuts in powdered sugar

Marzipan Menorah

1 pkg. marzipan
Food coloring

1. Divide the marzipan in half. Now split one half into 3 pieces, and make each piece a different color.
2. Roll each piece into 3 snake-y shapes. Twist the 3 snakes together to made one long braided piece, and cut the braid into 2 or 3 candles.
3. Color the other half of the marzipan yellow and roll out the menorah branches and stand.
4. Add the candles to the menorah
5. Listen to cheers for your work!

CHEF'S TIP

Marzipan becomes soft and sticky as it gets warmer, so try to work as quickly as you can. Also, you won't want to move your Chanukah menorah once it's finished, so after you've made all the parts, put it together in a pretty plate or on top of a cake.

How to Make a Quick Driedel!

(TRACE)

1. Draw a circle with a design and color it in.
2. Cut it out and stick a match or toothpick right through the middle.
3. Spin it and watch what happens to your design as it turns around and around! Here's an example:

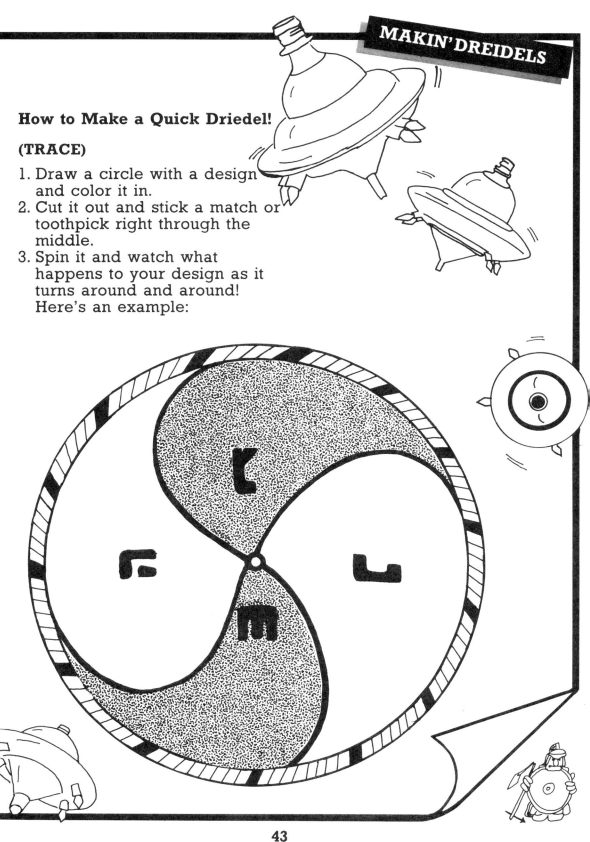

ANSWERS

Page 2 Password Puzzle The words are: **menorah light eight chanukah dreidel candle** and **maccabee**. The password is **miracle**.

Page 3 Mystery Man His name is **Antiochus Epiphanes**.

Page 7 Puzzling Pictures a. **plate of latkes** b. **menorah** c. **dreidel** d. **present**

Page 8 & 9 Family Facts The symbol of Judah is a **lion**. The names on the family tree are **Mattityahu, Jonathan, Yochanan, Elazar, Simon** and **Judah**

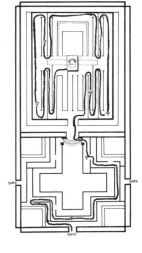

Page 10 & 11
Maccabee Maze

Page 15
Temple Search

Page 12 & 13 Chanukah Race

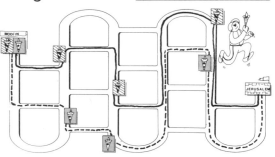

Page 17
Candle Crossword

Page 18 & 19 In the Dungeon The inquisitors are carrying a trumpet, baseball glove, knitting, an umbrella and a brush. Also they didn't have electricity so the light bulbs and wall clock shouldn't be there.

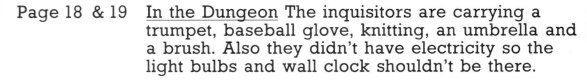

Page 20 Countin' Countries **South America Morocco Egypt France Italy Holland**

Page 21 Portrait Puzzles

It's **Christopher Columbus**

Page 35   Siberian Scene

Page 40   Chanukah Crossword

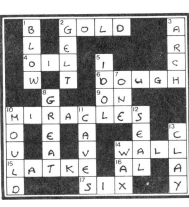

Also available from Scopus Films **ANIMATED HOLYDAYS** series – entertaining and educational childrens' books, films and games on the Jewish festivals:

Books

THE ANIMATED MENORAH Two children travel through time and space on a magic dreidel. Their adventures with Judah the Maccabee, George Washington, a Russian refusenik and many others tell the story of Chanukah.

THE ANIMATED ISRAEL A fable about friendship, separation and reunion. The story, in rhyme, parallels the history of the Jewish people.

THE ANIMATED MEGILLAH A Purim adventure. Palace plots and intrigue in the capital of ancient Persia. The evil Haman plans to gain wealth and power by wiping out the Jews.

THE ANIMATED HAGGADAH A beautifully illustrated Haggadah for children, with complete Hebrew text and notes for parents and teachers.

Videos

THE ANIMATED HAGGADAH An innovative video that brings the Passover story to life through vivid clay animation. A contemporary child at the Seder table dreams he is in the land of the Pharoahs.

FLIEGEL'S FLIGHT, A BIRD'S-EYE VIEW OF JEWISH HISTORY A cartoon bird takes two children on a tour through Jewish history. Archive film, cartoons, special effects and an original musical score based on well-known Jewish and Israeli tunes give an overview of Jewish history from Abraham to contemporary Israel. Can be used in conjunction with the Animated Israel book.

Games

HANNUKIT An all-in-one box of eight presents, one for each night of Chanukah. Includes the Animated Menorah book!